T0365544

Awakening

M. L. McDonald

Order this book online at www.trafford.com
or email orders@trafford.com

Most Trafford titles are also available at major online book retailers.

Printed in the United States of America.

ISBN: 978-1-4669-7237-7 (sc)
ISBN: 978-1-4669-7236-0 (e)

Trafford rev. 03/04/2013

 www.trafford.com

North America & international
toll-free: 1 888 232 4444 (USA & Canada)
phone: 250 383 6864 ♦ fax: 812 355 4082

Contents

Foreword

This collection of stories represent a woman's journey into open sexuality within the confines of a relationship with a 'sexual deviant'. She didn't do anything that was outside of her own desires and was in no way coerced into anything she found abhorrent. While I realize this may have some tinges of a dominant/submissive relationship, the collection was written before I read 50 shades. It is a work of fiction, I do have a muse and he paints some very vivid pictures. Without you MickeyD, this would not have been possible.

I had fun writing them and I really hope you have fun reading them. I also hope they can cause that curl in your pelvis that they never fail to do for me too!

I am grateful to 'The Gang', my models, my various editors and encouragers along the way. The photos were done to depict a central part of each story, tastefully, I hope. Thanks www.geraldgentlesphotography.com, I loved working with you and look forward to more of our pictorial journey.

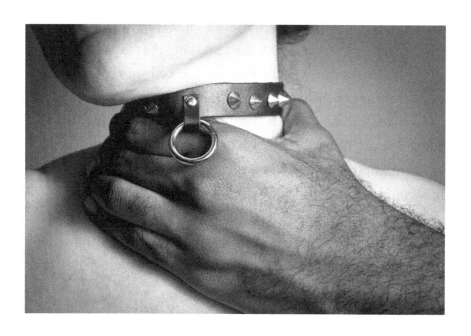

Blindfold

I'm nervous, not knowing what to expect.

He has given me a short tight black leather skirt that barely covers my butt and a bustier to match that barely covers my breasts, my abdomen bare. The heels are 5 inches high, full of crisscrossing straps, black, shiny and gorgeous. Ooooooh, where ever did he find these I wonder, yet again? I have on no other jewelery or embellishments other than the half inch thick black collar around my neck.

Slightly biting the lower right corner of my dark red lips, I await his arrival on pins and needles. Do I REALLY want to do this? Can I survive this night? What has he planned? Will I enjoy this? What the hell am I doing???

I am poised on the edge of the sofa, waiting, waiting . . . . is this a part of the scene? To build the anticipation to unbearable proportions? I look at the clock and realize a mere 2 minutes has passed and I sigh.

I begin to wonder, where is he?

When I hear the key in the lock my breath hitches in my throat. I raise my right hand to the collar, running my fingers over it and the metal fixture for the chain, wondering for the umpteenth time, do I really want to do this? I close my eyes, breathe deeply asking for the inner strength to go through with this. We've discussed it countless numbers of times, laughing and sharing our expectations, what it means to each of us and more currently, our joy in the moment that is finally becoming a reality.

The door opens.

He steps into the room, our eyes meet. I smile nervously at him and I stand up, carefully, still maintaining eye contact. He closes the door and walks slowly towards me, that MickeyD grin I looove so much breaking out all over his face, he breaks eye contact to look at the masterpiece that he has orchestrated and taking in a big breath, he slowly blows it out, eying me and my outfit salaciously. Hmmmmm he says and reaching into his pocket, takes out a black silk strip of cloth and the chain.

I open my mouth to ask him a question . . . . shhhhhh he says gently resting his right index finger on my lips, do you trust me he whispers in my ear while caressing my left thigh below the skirt. He slips his hand between my thighs and I groan as he runs his fingers over my clit, pushing against my lips, involuntarily my legs part. My eyes close and my breathing quickens and I feel that usual tightening of my breasts and clenching of my pelvis and that rush of warmth that comes to my centre. Yes, I whisper while nodding my head, no doubts, no second thoughts. He pulls his hand away and I sigh.

I hear the rattle of the chain and I open my eyes as he slips it on the metal fixture at the front of the collar. Come he says gently. The length of the chain is no longer than 3 feet, so we are relatively close to each other as he leads us through the door. I walk docilely behind him, hands at my sides, carefully on these heels. We enter a room filled with people and I look around, they are all drinking and eating, relaxed, chatting and laughing. Self consciously, I tuck my hair behind my ears. Standing tall and silent looking around at the people in the room, I recognize no one, make no eye contact.

Come, he says and we walk to the bar and he asks for a glass of red wine. Drink it he says and I sip it, it's a nice wine, not too dry and not too sweet, room temperature, just the way I like it. We stand while I drink slowly and I begin to feel the effect of the alcohol in my system almost immediately. My vaginal lips begin to swell and I begin to feel wet, my breathing increases and my heart rate goes up. I can feel my face begin to flush.

He takes the empty glass from me and leads me to a firm leather sofa, empty and not pushed against the wall and tells me to kneel on it at the edge, facing the back bending over almost on all fours, I comply and he attaches the chain to a hook on the wall. He rests my hands on the back of the sofa. He moves to stand behind me and begins to caress my outer thighs and my sides the way he knows I like, rubbing at my now super sensitive skin, softly here and a little harder there. My breathing increases and I can feel my juices begin to flow. I bite my lower lip and I hang my head down. My hair forms a curtain on either side of my face. He moves his hand between my legs pushing them apart slightly and enters me with his fingers, I groan softly and begin to move my hips with the motion of his hand. His fingers set up that rhythm, in and out, rubbing at my G-spot incessantly. He groans as I squirt into the palm of his hand and I smile a little to myself. He withdraws his fingers, licking at them as he always does and wipes some of the liquid on my thighs and I sigh with regret.

He pulls the silk out of his pocket and ties it on from behind, covering the top half of my face and asks if I can see anything, I say no. He moves the hair from my face on one side and kisses me on the neck, flicking his tongue against me and I lean into him. I can hear people moving around and the room goes silent. He talks softly to me as he moves to stand on the other side of the sofa facing me, he places his hands on mine and kisses me on the mouth, our tongues intertwine and I suck slightly at his. I feel a caress on my left outer thigh and I shy away. Easy he says to me, I'm here and I settle down . . . . the caress comes again and another on the other side, soft hands lightly rubbing my thigh, a harder more calloused hand on the other side. I close my eyes behind the mask and begin to FEEL with out seeing, I know he is there and I feel safe, knowing he would never allow harm to come to me and that nothing would be done that I don't want done.

And then other hands begin to touch my breasts, softly caressingly all over, a bit harder there and softer else where. Some hands feel soft and some feel roughened, the sensations come at me from all sides. I stop trying to separate them. They are pushing up my skirt and they grab at my butt, caressing in some places and soft pinches in others. Pulling the bustier away from my breasts, the hands rub and caress my nipples, tugging and pulling at them. Caresses to my back and breasts, sides, belly, thighs, inner and outer, I begin to writhe to these caresses that seem to set up a cadence in my body, all in sync, all for my pleasure. I feel fingers enter me still wet from him, one then two, nothing to hurt or too rough. My legs open wider as they begin to move in and out, rubbing at my G-spot, I feel another caressing my clit softly and most erotically, is that a tongue? Rubbing or licking sooo insistently, softly at first then harder as I move into it. I groan softly as I come and my hands clench the sofa, which he can feel under his. He sees the movements of my pelvis and hears the sounds I make that are exclusively mine. He can see the expression on my face as they keep up the caresses, the tongues and the fingers as I come again and again.

I feel his hands squeeze at mine and he kisses me softly on the lips, that is his area as we agreed, none other to encroach there. So I know it is him. He can taste the wine on my mouth and I taste me on his. He puts his hand on my head and I feel when he places his thumb on my lower lip and says to me, I'm soooo hot for you and I open my mouth as he enters me and without hands suck at him, moving my head until he comes, thrusting in my mouth and I swallow him into myself.

As he withdraws, all the hands leave me, quivering and drained. I wait docilely as he fixes my clothes, still on all fours. I can hear the sounds begin again as he picks me up gently and takes me back to our room, me still blindfolded and trusting, knowing that he will return me to our harbour of safety.

The Friend

The night is cool and the sounds of the crickets loud and constant. A slight wind is blowing, bringing with it the smell of the sea and the sound of the waves on the beach far below. A bright full moon shines enticingly above the horizon and reflects on the distant sea.

We are comfortable with each other, the three of us, as we chat and laugh about some of our past individual experiences and some of the present ones we share. Stories are repeated sometimes ended by each other as we recall past interactions. The conversation flows along with the wine we had consumed with dinner and I begin to feel somewhat tipsy. I am sitting close to him and he is rubbing his hands on my feet that are resting in his lap, rubbing against his crotch and belly as I always do. The friend sits opposite us and watches with affection and some envy. The obvious love and togetherness we share is something to behold and never fails to bring regret for opportunities missed and past loves let go. The conversation continues and we mellow as the moon rises some more.

The helper comes and clears the table and unobtrusively asks if we needed anything else? No thanks, we say in unison. She says good night then and that she'd see us at breakfast and leaves.

It's a good combination, we're comfortable with each other having spent countless hours like this, just chatting and generally enjoying each others company. As he rubs my feet and I feel the vibration of his conversation and laughter through my feet, I begin to feel like a moment out of time has arrived and the decision is all up to me. And this would be all about me, for me to experience and for us to do it together. I recall some of the discussions we've had about potential 3-sums and what it would entail and what we would look for, the synergy amongst all the participants we would hope for. Is it now I wonder? When it comes down to it, is the time really now? Is there a better time? A different 'other'?? I know the friend is up for it, I know he is . . . . am I up for it too?

So many things swirling through my mind as he rubs my feet and caresses my legs and further afield. The usual feelings he incites in me are evident in the heaviness in my abdomen, the tightness in my nipples and the beginning of the wetness he never ceases to bring by his mere touch.

I get up to go to the bathroom and they continue chatting about some issues that are current. I hear them laughing and commenting on some trivial acts that we all are privy to. I take in a deep breath and decide to take the plunge.

I pick up one of the larger cushions from the sofa inside and walk back to them. I place it on the table in front of the friend and without looking at either of them, I begin to take my clothes off. The friend can't take the eyes off me as I disrobe.

He looks at me in some surprise as this was not anything that was even hinted at before this action that so obviously means the time IS now.

One time deal I say, never to be spoken of by either of you . . . . they both quickly and eagerly agree, looking at each other.

I sit on the cushion atop the table and he can see the arch of my back as I sit in front of the friend, feet braced against the edge of the table, I spread my legs wide open enough for the friend to see the glistening from the moon light that is there, ready for this act to be consummated. I lean back, bracing on my elbows, throwing my head back. Without hesitation, the friend's head bends and the tongue begins to lick at my clit with some butterfly touches that drives me instantly wild. Darting in and out, to and fro, across it, up and down, tonguing the piercing. He watches for a moment, the intense look on my face with my eyes closed, he knows I am feeling everything acutely that the friend is doing. He moves to stand up behind me, taking the weight of me onto his chest. He leans into my neck and begins to kiss and suck at me, flicking his tongue and I throw my head against his shoulder, groaning with pleasure at the onslaught that comes at me from all sides. I brace into his chest as he supports my back. His hands reach around me and begins to stroke my breasts that are so sensitive normally, thus arousing me further carrying me closer to the edge. He runs his hands along the side of my abdomen and back up to my breasts, up and down.

He bends around me and takes one nipple into his mouth, swirling it around his tongue, sucking it firmly and wetting it, moving to the other breast, as he plays with it with his tongue,

9

he slides his hand over to the wetness that was his mouth before. Oh God I groan, pushing myself more firmly into his mouth, pushing his head more into contact with my breast. He knows this is one of my most erogenous zones and his attention causes a flood of fluid that comes into the friend's mouth. The friend makes a sound, lapping up this evidence of my arousal and plunges the tongue into me as far as is possible and my hips rise off the table into the tongue, fingers come into play and two fingers stroke my G-spot and the tongue, the clit and the play with the piercing is such an erotic thing. I writhe into the friend and my hips begin to move, maximizing the action of the tongue and the fingers as they plunge in and out, full of my wetness.

I push harder against him and give a slight squeak as I come, my hips bring me into the most contact with the friend's mouth. The convulsions that come with it are a sight to behold as the moon light ripples across my abdomen and the scar that signifies the death of a hope long realized but never to be fulfilled.

I grip his arms tightly, breathing fast, he inhales my orgasm into himself through my mouth and this kiss that seems endless and all the more enticing as my body spasms. The fact that he is not the cause of this makes him love me all the more because I chose to share this moment among those in whom I have the most trust.

The Gazebo

Dinner was the usual semi-filled dining area with all the noise and friendships forged in a short space of time by like minded people that are together for now. Everybody was in their usual state of undress. I had on a long flowing skirt and a short blouse, he ordinary shorts and a t-shirt. I could hear people talking about my awakening and that I was the leather girl from several nights back and how erotic it was for them to be a part of my experience. Hanging my head down, I feel some embarrassment being a normally private person sexually and he can see and feel my discomfort. Oh sweetie he says softly, it's ok, rubbing his hand along my forearm, I smile as he says, it was a beautiful thing. I inhale deeply, raise my head and look deeply into his eyes and sigh. Yes, it was a beautiful thing.

We hang around a little longer, eating dessert and drinking coffee. As we leave the dining area holding hands and smiling at each other, I look around at the other people there, he pulls me close and as we walk pass the main pool. We stop to stare at the sea and the moon as it reflected on it. Such a nice holiday, something we have talked about for years. Sun, sea, frolic. One less thing on the to-do list.

We start back in the direction of the room listening to the merry-making and laughter in the swim up bar, the party is in it's usual full swing. He looks at me and I shake my head, no. OK he mouths as we avoid walking in that direction, taking the scenic route.

He puts his arm around my shoulder and rubs against my nipple, that instantly tightens in anticipation, he hears the hitch in my breathing and smiles to himself. We stop on the path and he turns me toward him slowly, I look up at him and his head comes down and our lips touch, sweetly at first and then harder. Our tongues intertwine and the kiss that started out as a meeting of our lips becomes more erotic. He reaches around for my butt and I go up on the tips of my toes while putting my arms around his shoulders. Knowing I have on no underwear, he pulls the skirt up, moving his hand to caress and stroke me, skin to skin. I make a sound deep in my throat and I can feel his response to me rub against my abdomen.

He raises his head and looks around spying a gazebo just off the path, we've passed it countless numbers of times and he knows there is a seat that runs around it on the inside and cushions strewn on the floor. He picks me up and takes me inside. It is semi-dark in there, slivers of light come through the leaves that surround it. We can hear people walking on the path we just left.

He puts me to sit on the seat and kneels in front of me, I open my legs to accommodate him and he moves into the crevice created. I rest my hands on his shoulders and he runs his hands up my sides and slips his fingers under the edge of my blouse and begins to rub my nipples with his thumbs. I groan with pleasure, gripping his shoulders. He kisses my abdomen, tonguing my navel and the ring that dwells there. My head falls forward and my hair brushes against his head and face. He feels my breathing increase and I begin to fidget, my legs moving restlessly rubbing up and down his sides and my pelvis begins to rock. I reach down and begin to caress his nipples through the shirt and run my hands along his sides.

He pushes my skirt up above my legs and thighs caressing my soft and smooth legs. I flex my feet to tip-toes and push my pelvis forward to the edge of the seat. My feet come up to rest on the edge of the seat, opening myself to him in the widest possible fashion, he breathes in deeply and inhales my scent, he can see the wetness that is already there. Needing no encouragement, he dips his head to taste me. I groan aloud and my head falls back. I grip the slats behind me that makes up the walls of the gazebo and I push myself into his face. He tongues me slowly and sucks at my wetness and runs his tongue around my clit softly, I hold my breath as his next move is to plunge his tongue as far as possible into me. As I scream softly, my pelvis rises off the seat into his face and he pushes open my legs as far as they can go, he reaches above to fondle my breasts and feels the wetness that comes out of me into his mouth . . . . hmmmmm he says and swallows my sweetness.

He takes his right hand and rubs it against me, wetting his fingers and he plunges two of them into me, still sucking at my clit, I inhale sharply and barely hear the people around us talking and watching us. The in and out motions of his hands causes me to undulate along with them, thrusting to meet him every time, he groans as I squirt once, twice into his hand and he stops and looks into his hand, fingers still in me, barely able to see the wetness in the low light. He withdraws his fingers and licks his hand with his eyes closed, tasting my familiar juices.

He is aware of the audience we have drawn, hears the comments of their observations, I am glassy eyed and look at him trustingly, a what next question in my eyes.

He opens his zipper and pants waist and they fall below his knees, I lean forward and touch him running my hand along the length of him and as he feels my familiar touch, inhales sharply as I guide him into me. He groans at my tightness and the oh so wetness of me and he falls into my depths without thought. I thrust forward to take him and he feels like he's home. I wrap my legs around his waist, pulling him into me tighter. You fill me up, I whisper and he withdraws slightly and enters me again, I thrust my pelvis towards him and he stops.

Looking at me as I watch him.

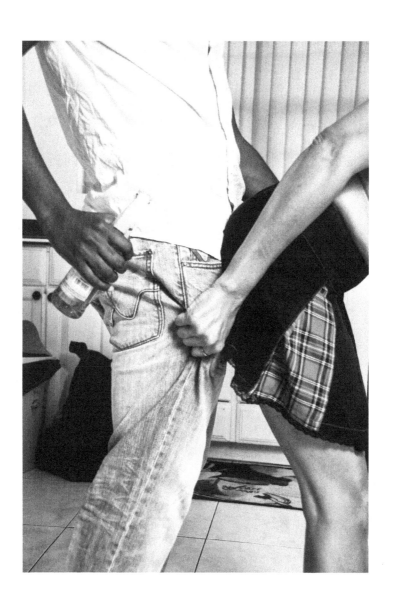

The Grind

The invitation to the party came as a by the way as my friend was going and asked me if I wanted to go also. He said go, he wouldn't be able to go with me to this one. I didn't much like going to parties without him, but decided well, since my friend needed the company and I was at loose ends anyway, so why not? If I had enough to drink and got really wild, I would dance seductively with some man there, grinding he always called it. I hadn't done that in a while. The feeling of power I had over the men gave me a high and was such a huge turn on . . . . for both of us, me in the act and for him when I told him about it. It puzzled me sometimes, the view he had on me with other men, but to each his own I thought, shrugging my shoulders.

The night came around and he was out like he said, I got ready to go and picked up my friend. We both dressed casually and comfortably, I in a skirt and my friend in jeans. It took a while for the party to start to swing and two watered down apple vodka and cherry juice later I was goood to go. There weren't many unattached men there, they came in groups some with females and they tended to stick together. As I danced and gyrated to the music and the pumping bass that I could feel resonating in my body, I looked up and made eye contact with a guy across the terrace. Ooooooh, he was fine looking, not too muscular, broad shoulders, little above medium height and well built. I continued to dance and enjoy the music and looked up again to see him watching me. This happened a couple more times and eventually I watched out the corner of my eye as he made his way over to me.

He stepped up in front of me and said hi, I've been watching you and I like your style. He had the most gorgeous smile, full and all over his face. I looked up at him and smiled back and said, well that is a new pick up line if ever I heard one. He laughed and told me his name, I reciprocated. My friend came and looked him over, ever vigilant of my virtue and I indicated to her, it's cool.

We started to dance together, exchanging information as the music allowed, I explained I was otherwise taken but wanted a night out and so came because my friend asked me to. He said ok, he was in a similar situation and understood the unspoken rules of our interaction. He moved to stand behind me and as the popular dance hall song Dumper Truck belted out the speakers, I smiled to myself and started to rub my butt against him. He inhaled sharply and moved forward into the grind. He rested his hand on my abdomen pulling me towards him more firmly and I gripped him on the pants leg opposite to his hand, pulling him into more contact with me.

As we moved to the rhythm of the music, I could feel his response to me, I could feel his breathing become more laboured and his evident state of arousal was unmistakable in the small of my back, I myself began to feel aroused, and I began to feel my juices flowing. Hoping it doesn't run down my leg, I smiled to myself, knowing just who was going to benefit from this when I got home. I dropped my head forward and bent from my waist, hair forming a curtain around my face. Enhancing the movement of my butt against his crotch, he placed one hand on my neck and the other on my hip to bring me into better contact with him and so we remained for a while, my hips moving to the music, he reciprocating grind for grind. Changing positions ever so often, but always that vital contact.

When the music changed, we change only the rhythm of our gyrations, encouraging each other to express ourselves and our obvious lust through the music. People stared at us, this couple who only needed to take their clothes off to consummate their union. I closed my eyes to enhance the feeling and I brought my hand up and placed it behind his neck, he ran his hand down my torso and I inhaled sharply which he could feel through his hand.

When I open my eyes I see him standing almost behind a column watching us, hands in his pockets. I don't acknowledge him but return to my newly discovered friend who while not knowing me, is capable of arousing me in the dance.

At the end of the set, I say to him, I thoroughly enjoyed myself, to which he bows from the waist, takes my hand and kisses the back of it. The pleasure was all mine he says. We smile at each other. I say to my friend, I soon be back and walk to the parking lot, knowing he is following me.

When I get to the car in the secluded dark parking lot, he is right behind me and I can feel the heat of his body, smell his familiar scent and feel his arousal, it is such a palpable thing.

He is breathing heavily. He grabs me on either side of my waist, holding me firmly almost roughly against him, I feel him soooooo hard against my back and I reach around behind me to grasp at his hardness. I rub my hand against the fullness of him and he bites me on my shoulder into my neck and I inhale sharply. He grinds himself roughly into my back groaning with his desire. He grabs my breasts, tweaking my nipples and roughly rubbing them almost painfully and I groan as the sensations become almost unbearable. I rub my hands against him harder and he thrusts against me enhancing his arousal.

He shoves the skirt up above my waist while fumbling to open his zipper and waist, I brace my hands against the bonnet of the car, oh so ready to receive him and I bend forward and raise one foot onto the bumper of the car as he pushes himself into me. I am so wet with desire for him, he slides in effortlessly.

Hmmmmmmmmmm, I groan pushing myself forcefully back onto him. He enters me with such abandon it heightens my need for him. I am so ready for him and he for me, as we dance this dance of unadulterated animal lust. And I feel the build up of sensations as he plunges into and out of me while I match his movements, he grips my side with one hand and reaches around to rub my clit roughly with the other. The piercing causes the sensations I feel to be so acute it sends me over the edge immediately. As I come and the spasms begin, I groan as I do and quicken my movements against him prolonging the feeling of my orgasm, he says I'm gonna come too and I respond, oh yes. He does that last heavy thrust, grasping my hips tight against him spasming and groaning as he spills himself into me.

Bondage

We have decided to take the afternoon from work, eating lunch at separate times and venues and to meet up at the hotel. I arrive first and book us in, go to the room and take a shower. He told me to lay on the bed without clothes and wait on his arrival. I text the room number to him as we agreed, no contact should be made, just so I wouldn't question him to death as is my wont, he admonished me not to talk to him.

I strip the top cover and sheet off and arrange the pillows at the top of the bed. Not talking to him however does not stop the questions I have in my head as I lay there, the TV off, no other sounds but that of the central air in the room and external traffic noises. The bed is comfortable and the sheets white and thick. What on earth has he planned to do day? I agreed to be blindfolded, and maybe bound. The safe word already agreed upon, I know he won't harm me, but man, what does he have in his mind to subject me to?? The upright struts of the four poster bed glare at me and I look at them with some trepidation. We've talked about this scene sooooo many times, and the variations sometimes I didn't find too appealing, but since trust is the name of this game, I decide to give him the go-ahead but within certain boundaries, for now.

Ooooooh boy, where is he? I can almost begin to feel myself hyperventilating in anticipation and feel my heart rate increasing. I almost feel sick with anticipation. I hear the door open and he walks in with a bag in his hand. He smiles at me, puts the bag on the desk and starts to take his clothes off, folding them and resting them on the chair. We're looking at each other, making eye contact and he says nothing, I bite my lower lip and follow his instruction not to speak. He walks to the bathroom and I hear the shower going, then the water is turned off and I can hear the shuffling of him drying off. He comes out with the bath robe on and sits on the end of the bed, he runs his hand on my feet and caresses me up to my knee and thigh. I half close my eyes and look at him. He loses himself in the caressing, up and down my legs and thighs, around my feet. I begin to feel that heaviness in my pelvis, my nipples tighten and that familiar wetness comes on me.

He stands up and moves towards the bag, indicating to me that I am not to say anything and reaches into the bag and pulls out a mask and two lengths of black silk. I look at him and he approaches me. He takes my left hand and ties my wrist to the left upright of the bed frame and then takes my right hand tying my wrist to the other side. I look at him and he says nothing, he bends over to put on the mask and I am now in total darkness and restrained to the bed by my wrists, we had discussed it before not to bind my legs, this time.

I feel when he gets up from the bed and I hear him rustling around, what is he doing I wonder?

I feel something cold dripping on my upper abdomen and I take in a sharp breath in as it runs down into my navel, it smells like wine. I feel when he places a hand on the bed and his weight comes down and I jump when I feel his tongue lick at what now is in my navel and follows the trail upward. My nipples tighten so hard they hurt begging him to take them into his mouth. Hmmmmmmmm he says, barely brushing his tongue against them, he breathes on the dampness he has created, I almost scream in frustration. He keeps blowing on them for a while and I begin to writhe with need.

He runs his hand lightly up my legs and thighs, butterfly touches, barely in contact with my skin, skirting my centre deliberately, up my sides and on my abdomen. Man, I think to myself, I'm not doing this again . . . . This is torture, and he has not yet begun. I thrust upward to where I think his hand maybe and he laughs softly . . . . Patience he says.

He flexes my knees and hips, and pushes them open as much as I can manage and leaves me like that for a minute or two, I breathe heavily in anticipation for whatever he has decided and then I feel the bed sink between my openness. And he blows on me softly causing me to inhale sharply and groan, I become so wet with need for him, he can see it oozing out of me. Trying to make contact with him, I thrust my hips forward and the restraints pull against my wrists and stops my motion to get closer to him.

He laughs, knowing just what he is doing to me and his tongue darts out, gently touching my wetness and brushes lightly against my clit, this time I groan aloud, he touches me again softly and I begin to thrust toward him in agony of want and need. He pushes his tongue in and sucks lightly, more for his want than for mine and I groan louder. He tongues the piercing gently and amplifies the feeling by pushing the ring in and out of the channel with his tongue rubbing against the nerve. I buck against him, asking without words to intensify the action. He pulls back and I feel the most incredible disappointment. He moves around on the bed and I feel more fluid drip onto me, running down my clit and between my butt cheeks and he lightly licks it off as I attempt to get him to apply more pressure.

I feel him place his fingers at the entrance to me, breathing on me heavily, still licking at the residual fluid that is now mixing with my own wetness. I writhe my hips begging him to enter me with my motions, he knows what I am is asking and deliberately avoids doing that. He barely pushes his fingers into me curving them upward as he heads for my G-spot, just at the entrance and I buck at the restraints, raising off the bed and pushing my pelvis towards him. He sees my wetness increase as I plead without words for him to push his fingers into me.

I moan with my unfulfilled desire for him and beg silently to give me what I'm asking. As he lightly fingers me, he knows that is not what I am seeking and he maintains his subtle actions, I moan and gyrate and he feels my wetness against his hand as my muscles stiffen and again another jet of my oh so sweet fluid squirts out of me, he closes his eyes with his own desire reaching a breaking point and he contemplates giving me what I want, as for him, this is a sweet torture as well.

He moves to kneel between my legs and I sense that he is almost at his breaking point and I take my legs and begin to rub them against his side, using my feet to caress his back and sides, he moves forward to enter me and I can feel him just against my entrance. He rubs his stiffness into my wetness, up and down and holds himself still as I use the motion of my hips to rub harder against him, he grips my thighs and moves my hips with him still resting at the entrance. I open my legs to encourage him to enter me and in trying to gain access to his length I pull against the restraints and move my hips as far down onto him as it permits. He holds his breath as he struggles not to enter me and watches my face as it expresses my desire for him.

You know, I begin to say hoarse with lust for him and he says Shhhhhhhh . . . . and I quiet and wait.

Falling Star

The room is open on all sides with huge picture windows and the breezes blowing in whips the sheer white curtains into a frenzy carrying with it the smell of the ocean and the sounds of the waves as they crash on the cliffs below. We needed this break from reality, a slice of heaven in the normal everyday work world pressures. Things being so hectic as we went through day to day issues, even as we tried to make our own moments of togetherness, life just didn't always do what we wanted it to do. As we were driving down, we had seen a falling star streaking across the sky and he had laughed and pointed saying, look, make a wish . . . .

Four days of heaven . . . .

I had begged him please, no extraneous anything, just the two of us enjoying each other in whatever form he wanted. He had laughed softy and said, okay mam, not a problem. Now that I thought about it, smiling to myself, any form HE wanted could be a dangerous thing. We were so tired the night before when we had gotten in, it was open up the windows and then straight to sleep, curled up around each other. I had sensed when he had gotten up earlier, kissed me on the cheek, saying sleep on sweets, I soon come back.

I look out through the front of the room and can see the sea over the low wall surrounding the property, blue and endless, the strip of grass from the edge of the verandah to the wall is so green and beautiful in the morning sun. I stretch while arching my back, making that little cat like sound as I normally do.

I get up and search the bag for that wrap I had packed and walk into the bathroom to put on sun screen and brush my teeth. I am feeling hungry and wonder where he might have gotten to. As I step out of the bathroom I can hear cutlery and people talking outside on the verandah where the table is set up. I look up and see him through the curtain with some one else setting up the table for breakfast. I walk over and push the curtain aside to go out onto the verandah, saying good morning. He's dressed casually and looks up, smiling, he holds out his hand to me, I walk over to him kissing him lightly on the lips and sticking my tongue into his mouth as he bends his head towards me. I rub my thumb on this hand and move to sit at the table. Hmmmmmmm, this smells good I say.

We eat leisurely, chatting and laughing about stuff, some of our work related issues and generally about life, as is the usual, there is never a lull in our conversation. My feet are resting in his lap rubbing his thighs and belly as always, I look over at the sea and inhale deeply, loving the feel of the moment. The person returns to pick up the dishes and we sit there a while longer sipping at our coffee while he caresses my legs and feet.

We get up and make our way down to the beach, being the middle of the week, we are alone there and decide to whole body sun. We mutually apply sunscreen and lay about for a while and swim and cool off, sun some more. Through out the day there are bits of teasing and caressing, light kisses and signs of affection and muted lust between us. We caress at each others erogenous zones, breasts, necks, feet, smalls of backs, sucking and kissing. As our desire for each other builds, we each back away until it eases up, never carrying it to fulfillment. What a torturous way to spend the day.

Lunch is a fun affair with a lot of laughter and that undercurrent of lust, steamed fish and bammy the way we both like it. We decide to catch a siesta afterwards. The afternoon rain us heavy and the blue skies of earlier, darkened and gray. The curtains whip about in the wind and the sound of the rain on the roof is loud and rhythmic. I awoke lying on my stomach, to find him rubbing my back and stroking me softly between my legs, he could tell the second I woke up. I make to move and he stops my movement with a hand slightly on my leg . . . . hmmmmmmmm I think to myself, OK then. He begins to kiss me in that sink between my shoulder blades from the top down to the small of my back, he pushes one thigh up, opening me, while rubbing gently between my legs. I begin to move my pelvis, which he pushes w on, indicating I am not to move.

I groan with my frustration but keep still. He caresses me from my feet up ward with one hand while keeping up that butterfly caress to my centre and I begin to writhe with my need for him, small tiny movements as if I were forcibly restrained, griping at the pillow under my head. He places his hand under my pelvis, raising me slightly off the bed and I feel his tongue lick at me, I scream with the sensation and feel the warmth of my first set of juices come out, he groans as he licks at it but still he does not enter me.

He pulls me upright on the bed and uses a piece of silk to tie my hands to one of the four posts so that I am kneeling on the bed facing the post. He is behind me again and I feel my juices running down the inside of my thigh. He rubs his hand in it while moving my thigh to place my foot on the bed, opening me up for the taking. He swirls his hand around my entrance, rubbing at me gently and I buck against his hand trying to rub myself against him and he pulls away, I begin to pant in my agony of want and need as he begins again to kiss and suck lightly at my back and butt, lightly between my legs. And then he pushes 2 fingers up into me and more juices flow down his hand. He rubs at my G-spot and I begin to move as the restraints allow with the rhythm of his fingers. I feel him move to tongue my clit at the same time and as his tongue makes contact once, twice, I orgasm into his mouth. Hmmmmmmm he groans aloud, licking and sucking at me, taking in as much as he can. His tongue swirls around the piercing while his fingers begin to move, in and out, building the sensations back up again.

He releases the restraint and places me on my back, he kneels beside my face and I turn my head to take him into my mouth, I swirl my tongue against him and begin to move my head, gripping his thighs holding him steady, licking and sucking and he groans and calls my name aloud, he moves his hand and pushes his fingers into me again and begins to move them in and out with the same rhythm and motion I am using and I again feel that familiar wetness squirt against his fingers as my hips move to the rhythm of his fingers.

He pulls himself out of my mouth and moves between my legs, rubs himself against my wetness and I arch my hips to take him in. He pushes all the way into me and he stops looking down into my eyes and I return the gaze. I wrap my legs around him and we both sigh and continue the dance we started hours ago. The rain eases up as we thrust and move with our natural rhythm and I groan as I orgasm and he pushes hard into me as he comes. He collapses onto me and remains like that for a while, nuzzling my neck and giving me tiny kisses on my lips. He rolls us both over and as I rest my head on his shoulder he wraps his arms around me and we both fall asleep to the cadence of the rain and the rhythm of our slowing heartbeats.

Wish on a falling star . . . .

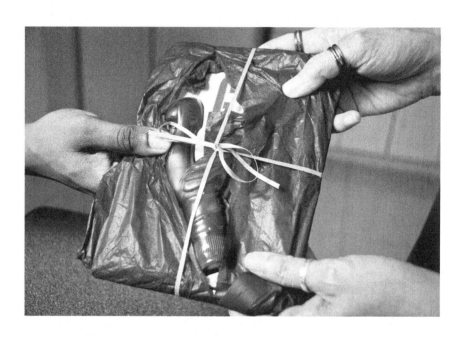

The Toy

The moonlight cast it's silvery light over everything, glinting on the sea, leeching out the colour and making things seem monochromatic. We're sitting on the low wall that circled the property, close together, shoulders touching, legs hanging down facing the sea, relaxing. Drinking wine and reminiscing about other wines we have had and what we were doing at those times. Some of them together, some at various times in our lives before we had gotten together.

We are holding hands, as my foot runs up and down his, our fingers intertwined and caressing each others palms and the backs of our hands. It was a slow easy day, filled with cat naps, moments of intense and moments of slow easy relaxed love making. And as per my request for nothing extraneous, we were happy and content in each others company. The conversation changed to other avenues of encounters we were interested in seeing and doing, I as always the shy one while he was more open with his sexuality. He made me laugh with some of the pictures he spun in my head and although not all of them appealed to me, some did on some level or another. Uuummmm hmmm, I say to some of his more outrageous encounters, groups, orgies, multiple men, swinging, obedience training . . . . I don't think sooooooo, I say more than once and we laugh familiarly and comfortably with each other.

He moves his hand to my back caressing me through the thinness of my blouse and I feel my nipples tighten in response and I sigh rubbing his thigh and pushing my hand further up, caressing his length through his shorts. He groans in response and turns to kiss me deeply while I reach up to hold his face firmly between my hands. Come he says helping me up from the wall and we walk towards the room stopping every few steps to grope at each other and stoke the fires of our mutual passion. He pushes his hand between my legs and I raise my thigh out of the way giving him better access and he rubs at my clit and centre and I groan aloud, while rubbing my hand against him up and down. He lifts me up laughing and saying we will never make it to the room at this rate and I respond, there are worse things than outside here. I lick at his neck and he inhales sharply.

As he steps up into the room and places me on the bed, I scoot up to the bedhead and prop myself up on the pillows stacked there. He says, I have something for you . . . . hmmmmmmmm I say, what could that be. He goes to his 'bag of tricks' and pulls out an irregularly shaped package, wrapped with a ribbon. I look at him and pull on the ribbon and the paper at the same time and pull out a 'G-spot clit hugger'. OMG I say laughingly, this is sooooo cool, as the other one we used to have had stopped working. Not quite the thing you take to an electronics store to try and repair, I had given up on replacing it for a while.

He sits at the foot of the bed facing me and says softly, use it for me. I look at him in surprise as I had never done this before and my face flushes. I look at the vibrator and open the plastic packaging, he takes it from me and cleans it with soap and water. I take my clothes off and return to leaning against the bed head. I take one of the firmer pillows and place it under my hips as he brings the toy to me and returns to where he was sitting before, directly in front of me. Turning it on, I feel the familiar humming and adjust the vibrations harder and faster. I open my legs, bending my knees and I place the tip of it on the piercing and inhale sharply as I feel the vibration through the ring straight to the nerves in my clit. Mmmmmmmmmm I say as I begin to move it up and down and swirl it around my entrance, dipping it into me, wetting it and smearing the wetness on to my clit and around. I do this over and over and he looks on and licks his lips. I plunge the long part of the toy into myself and turns the vibrating part onto my G-spot and I close my eyes while applying pressure to the toy enhancing the feel of the vibrating part. My hips begin to thrust against the toy as I move it in an out of myself and I apply the subtle pressure of the vibrating part against my G-spot, my legs open wider and I stiffen and groan as I orgasm. I pull it out and use the wet tip against my clit prolonging the intensity and length of it. Hmmmmmmmm I say as I open my eyes to see him watching my face and my actions so avidly.

He takes the toy from me and mimicking my movements, keeps rubbing my wetness all over my clit and centre. I moan again and move my hips for him to put it back into me and he desists, building my desire for release to unbearable proportions. As he toys with me, he himself is becoming more aroused as he watches me, writhing and moaning with desire.

He rubs it against my breasts, moving it around, slathering me with my own juices and the feel of the vibrations tightens my nipples into hard points of pure sensation going straight to my clit. He pushes the toy into me pushing the vibrator hard up towards my G-spot, keeping up the pressure and a flood of warmth comes out, wetting the pillow and his hand. He pulls the vibrator out and moves towards my open legs and glistening wetness. He leans over me kissing me deeply, our tongues meeting and sucking at each other, he runs his hands down my side and caresses my damp breasts and I arch into him rubbing my wetness against his length and he inhales and thrusts towards me.

He pulls back and reaches down to push his fingers inside me and begins that oh so familiar caressing of me inside. While our lips are locked, I reach down and caress his sides, rubbing at his nipples and butt, squeezing at it. I run my hands along his length, up and down, firmly and lightly caressing the tip, rubbing his own wetness against him. He bucks against my hands and groans, pulling away to ease up on the sensations building up in him. I spasm and squirt into his hand and he pulls his fingers out, licking at them.

I push him over onto his back and sit astride him with my back to him. I raise up slightly, grasp him and guide him into me, easing down onto him. He thrusts up into me, groaning aloud surrounded by the warmth and wetness that is me, leaning forward I grab his ankles and begin to rock my pelvis against him while pushing back onto him. He grasps my waist and helps my downward thrusts, I quicken against him as I orgasm and bear down rubbing hard against him as he comes into me.

The Hammock

There is a sense of good things coming to an end as tomorrow we get to go home . . . . yippeeeeee. It's been a great break from reality, all of what we wanted, needed and thought it to be. Recharge of our batteries and some well needed alone time. We decide to do this every 3 months, maybe not always for 4 days, but certainly a break spent in an off the beaten track sort of place.

We're laying on the beach, soaking up some sun, breakfast all done, the morning sunshine is warm, not overly hot and the sea is calm and clear. Our talk is of other places we may wish to go, perhaps none as laid back and carefree as this but certainly some places worthwhile exploring. This will always be our slice of heaven, and we vow to return. He rests his hand on my hip and I shy away from him, laughing and saying, mind you make me have outline of your hand as a tan line. He laughs saying, hmmmmmm, now that's an idea.

We frolic in the sea, the water cool and crisp after lying in the sun. Holding hands, we walk along the shore for a bit, looking at shells and the sea debris. I pick up a particularly pretty pink shell, saying I'm going to keep it as a memento of our time there. As the mid-day sun approaches, it begins to get hotter and we decide to go back to the room. We climb the steps to the outdoor shower, as he turns on the pipe I step under the spray screaming with laughter as the icy cold water hits my sun heated body. He laughs and begins to soap me up and he steps under the shower himself as well to wet his skin. As we get used to the temperature of the water, our motions become more seductive and caressing than functional. As we move our hands over each other, the slippery soap and lack of friction makes the sensations more acute. He turns me around to face the spray and I brace my hands against the shower wall in front of me and he runs his soapy hands up and down my back, dipping between my legs and I open up for him by raising one of my legs slightly. He bites me on my neck and I groan as he pushes his hand from behind to rub at my clit. The water is splashing all round us as he turns me around and puts more soap all over my breasts and abdomen, the slipperiness and the cold water as he swirls his hands on my body brings goose bumps to my skin. The cold water makes me wriggle and I step out of it, pushing him under.

I begin to soap him up from behind first, his back, butt and between, reaching to caress him, his thighs and legs, bending down to soap his feet which he raises for me in turn. I stand up and soap his head and neck and start to kiss him where I can reach, I turn him around and continue with his chest and abdomen, arms, using the soapy slithery feel to run my hands all over him. I begin to caress him, up and down his length, caressing the tip and below, washing him off. He inhales sharply as I bend my head and take him into my mouth, holding his thigh, keeping him immobile. As I take in the tip and swirl my tongue around him, I suck lightly and then push all of him into my mouth. He feels my throat muscles relax to take him in and the feel of the cold water on his skin and the warmth of my mouth is such a contrast in temperatures, he shivers. He groans as I repeat the action again and again.

He turns the water off and pulls me up onto his chest and we kiss hard, tongues intertwining, sucking hard at each other. I put my arms around his shoulders and flex my hip, bend my knee and wrap my leg around his thigh. He reaches down and rubs at my clit and the piercing and I buck against him. I reach down and begin to caress him along his length. He lifts me up and walks over to the hammock and he puts me to stand beside it. We reach for some towels and dry each other off lightly and he puts me to sit on one of the long sides. He kneels in front of me and pushes me to lie down, flexing my hips and putting the bottom of my feet on the edge. Gently swaying the hammock, he begins to play with my body, sucking on my breasts as the hammock moves towards him, and releasing me as it moves away. I put my hands above my head, gripping the edge of the canvas covering tightly. His for the taking.

He caresses my abdomen, rubbing his hands against my breasts and the motion of the hammock helps him. He rubs at my clit with his thumb and I brace my legs, he pulls my body more to the edge and in the same motion pushes his fingers into me. I groan as he begins his magic and in pushing the hammock away from himself, the in and out motions are exaggerated and helped. I writhe around on the hammock, but can not really thrust towards his hand. The sensations are increased by this and I feel the familiar warmth leave my body and he grunts when the fluid hits his hand.

He kneels down, his fingers still in me and licks at my clit, moving the piercing around and I raise my pelvis against his mouth as he licks at me, his fingers begin to move again, building up the sensations as he licks and sucks at me. I begin to get wetter and the action of his fingers and mouth causes another squirt of fluid. He groans and licks at it, taking his fingers out and I watch he licks at that too.

He stands up, pushing the hammock a little way away from him and rubs his tip against me. I move my pelvis up and down against him, rubbing my wetness onto him, and he groans as he pushes himself fully into me, pulling the hammock towards him. He begins to push the hammock away and pull it towards him, never that far as to come out of me and he intensifies the sensation by rubbing against my clit and the piercing when the hammock comes in. I arch my back at the same instant and he holds me against him each time the hammock comes towards him, holding the edge of the hammock, I move with him. We continue this motion as the hammock acts as that extra bit of pressure between us and I groan as I orgasm. He watches my face and the actions of my body and it pushes him over the edge and he comes into me, thrusting and stiffening as he falls on top of me, breathing heavily. I laugh while hugging and wrapping my legs around him and say, mind we bruk down this thing enuh, as the hammock sways on it's own.

Creaking in the mid-day sun.

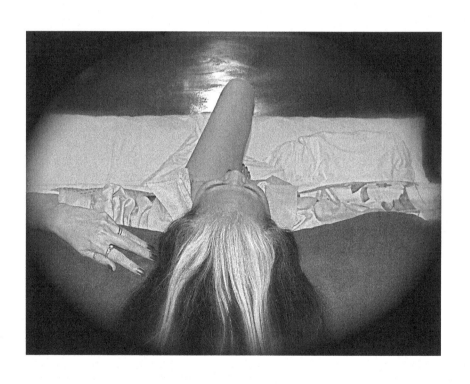

Unexpected

He always takes my breath away with his little half grin and the knowledge that he has something nefarious in mind for me is never far away in my thoughts. What now, I think as he comes through the front door with a brown paper bag in hand. Have I got something for you, he says smiling that mickeyD grin of his. More likely for you, I reply laughing. Hummmmmmmm, he says, how yuh know soh? I sigh mightily, rolling my eyes saying, oookay then, what is it this time? He laughs and says to me, after dinner my love.

Like I can REALLY concentrate on dinner now. The red wine was a dead give away, my word I think, what on earth has he in mind tonight? I drink sparingly as we eat and he encourages me, drink up man, drink up. What he need to drunk me off for? Hmmmmmmmm, maybe I would be better off catatonic. The wine starts to have it's usual affect, head little woozy, flushed, warm inside and ultra-horny. The down side is, wanting to sleep if I have had too much . . . . we sit and chat a bit, sharing bits and pieces of our day and the plans we have for the weekend. As usual, my feet are in his lap and he is rubbing them as he usually does, caressing my legs and feet. I run them up and down his thighs and rub at him through his pants, feeling the effect I have on him as he hardens. My skin is sensitive from the wine and seems to join the nerves from my feet straight to my center, which begins to swell and moisten. I start to move restlessly and he watches me, knowing just what effect he and the wine are having.

He shifts his legs open and pushes the chair further from the table and pulls me to stand in front of him, leaning me against the edge of table. I put my hands on his shoulders and begin caressing them through his shirt. He rests his hand on my lower abdomen and pushes it under my blouse, running his hand and fingers over my breasts and pinching and pulling slightly at my erect nipples, I inhale sharply as he kisses my belly just above my navel, sucking hard at the skin giving me a hickey that he knows I love so much. He takes his hand from my breasts and pushes the edge of my skirt up, caressing my legs, climbing up my thighs slowly. I take one foot off the floor and rest it on the outer edge of the chair, beside his thigh, opening up myself to him. He starts rubbing gently against my clit with his thumb and using the palm of his hand rubs against my wetness, I move my hips to intensify his touch and ease back to sit on the table. He pushes my skirt up further and dips his head between my legs, flicking his tongue at my clit and at the piercing and I push myself toward his mouth grinding myself into him. He grips my thighs on the outside and I put my hands on his head and back. My eyes close and the sensations build up as I caress his head while he moves it up and down to lick at me. He releases my thigh and he moves his hand and pushes his fingers into me, rubbing at my G-spot, insistently until he feels that familiar warmth hit his hand. He pulls his hand out, licking at it, face and beard damp with my wetness and looks at me as I open my eyes to gaze at him.

He stands up and takes my foot off the chair as we walk to the bedroom, arms around each other. We take off their clothes and get into the bed. I lie on my back, head on the pillows and he ties my wrists and ankles to the bed posts and dons my mask, hmmmmmm I say and close my eyes, turning my head to the side he last was. He goes silent and touches me fleetingly along my sides, up to my breasts, swirling around my nipples and back down. I strain against the ties seeking his touch as he silently continues what he knows is my torture. He rubs his fingers lightly against my clit, once, twice and I inhale sharply, groaning and arching my back. I feel when he reaches on the nightside table for something and listen to to the sound of a bottle opening and him rubbing his hands together. Then the warmth of some massage oil on my skin starts everything tingling where he touches and he proceeds to touch everywhere. I savour the sensations as he works his magic from the neck down, but never touching any of my erogenous now highly sensitive areas, I become almost sleepy with the effects of the wine and his massage. He removes his hands and I groan with the disappointment of something good ending and feel when he leaves the bed, hear the rustle of what I assume to be the 'brown paper bag' and wonder what he has up his sleeve.

He moves between my open legs, I feel more oil on my abdomen and he rubs it all over my centre and clit areas, around and up and down, and he pushes his fingers inside me while I writhe and move as much as I can with the restraints in place. He pulls his finger out, wet and slick with my juices and I feel him rubbing against my entrance. I raise my hips and push down and feel him push against me, but the feeling is odd and not LIKE him?? What on earth, I question aloud and he laughs. What are you up to, I ask and he pushes it in further, it is huge and I can feel it as it stretches me out to accommodate it. Mercy, I breath and he begins to work it in and slightly out, entering me in stages.

He releases one of the ankle restraints and pushes my hip up and open, and bends his head to lick at me. While he applies the pressure, he licks and sucks at my clit and the piercing, rolling it around on his tongue and I, initially uncomfortable begin to move with the motions he is inducing. Eventually he is able to fit it all in and as he continues to suck at me, he mimics the motion in and out, me moving with him as far as the restraints allow.

He feels the build up in my muscles as I near orgasm and he switches on the vibrator part of it, still sucking at me. The unexpected feel of the pulsing pushes me over the edge and I scream at the sensations while he continues to apply the pressure in and out, sucking at my clit and I sigh saying enough, please. My legs are trembling and I am panting while he turns it off and pulls it out, licking at my wetness while I spasm with each touch of his tongue.

Comfort

It's been a rough week, deadlines to be met, endless stress to complete the assignments and project, sorting out issues as they arise. I've been up and out of the house early and home late, meals on the run, days hectic.

It's Friday night, the event horizon is over. He came home early, talking to me on the phone as I drove home, keeping me company and congratulating me on a job well done. He has timed my arrival right, meets me at the door and helps me with my stuff, taking off my jacket while I kick off my shoes and sigh, wiggling my tired toes. He gives me a hug, standing still in the embrace for a while, he hands me a glass of red wine . . . . hmmmmmm I say, thanks and sip at it gingerly. For relaxation he says, smiling. He takes my free hand and pulls me toward the bedroom, unbuttoning my skirt and pulling at the zip, as I step out of it I see the rose petals scattered about the floor and on the bed, I turn to him with a half smile on my face and he leads me further toward the bathroom. I can see the glow through the door, flickering candle light and the smell of lavender perfumed air. He takes the glass and helps me out of the rest of my clothes while I pin up my hair. He leads me to the jacuzzi tub, with the steaming water swirling around, floating rose petals fragrant in the water.

Stepping down into the tub, he helps me to sit on the second lower step, handing me back the glass, I sigh with relaxation as the steaming water swirls around my body and I close my eyes with pure enjoyment. I feel him come up behind me and I half open my eyes and he feeds me some crackers with smoked salmon and cream cheese. Mmmmmmmmmm, nice. Sipping at the wine and eating as he feeds me, I begin to feel sleepy as the hot fragrant water swirls around me. I sense when he steps into the tub and sits behind me, his knees on either side of me. He pulls me back to lean on him. I put my arms around his knees and we begin to talk softly, mostly about getting our life back on it's usual keel. He nuzzles my neck as I tilt my head to the side and I feel that familiar response to him as tired as I am and I smile to myself, wine does it every time.

He begins slowly and firmly to massage my shoulders, right where those knots are that tense up under stress and I groan with their unwinding. He runs his hands that I love so much up and down my arms and shoulders and I close my eyes half drowsily. I feel when he eases up and reaches down to lift me out of the water, hands under my knees and under my arms, I rest my head against his chest. He wraps a fluffy warm towel around me and takes me over to a massage table he has set up to one side. Placing me on my tummy and turning my head to the side, he wipes the excess water off my back and legs, I sigh as he places that mask over my eyes blocking out my vision and allowing me to be more sensitive to touch. I hear when he opens the bottle of massage oil, squirting it on my skin. He rubs his hands into the oil and starts to massage my feet and legs. I sense when other people enter the room and feel when they also begin to massage the various areas of my back and shoulders, thighs and arms. Hmmmmmmmm I say as my muscles begin to relax and I feel like a limp noodle. My mind begins to wander and I feel so lethargic from those hands that know where to caress and how to apply pressure and softness where it is required.

As I relax and the stress leaches away, the effect of the wine and the scents, the caresses and the sheer multi-handed effects of their ministrations begins to bring a familiar warmth and moisture to my centre and my breathing increases. He kisses me on my cheek and whispers that he's gonna turn me over now. More oil is placed on my body and they begin again, this time he is by my head caressing my neck and shoulders, up and down my arms. He moves his hands to my breasts and the lack of friction with the oils and his hands, slippery and caressing makes me groan with longing and need. The other hands continue their massaging of my abdomen and thighs, legs and feet. He bends down, whispering in my ear, kissing me, running his tongue around and in my ear. Goose bumps come up on my skin and I shiver.

I feel when one of the other persons bends my knees and flexes my hips, rubbing my inner thighs while the other hands are caressing my legs and feet, hands reach under my butt and raise me off the table and I groan as I feel a tongue caress my clit oh so softly and deliberately, playing with the piercing. I begin to move my hips in time with the tongue as it moves up and down softly, side to side, sucking at the clit and moving the skin back increasing the sensitivity. As the pressure increases slowly I push down to enhance the feeling. The tongue slips into me, sucking at me and my wetness increases as I move with the sensations. The tongue moves back to my clit and fingers slide into and out of my wetness, rubbing at my G-spot.

He continues to caress my breasts as he knows this is one of my most sensitive spots and I arch my back and groan with pleasure as the sensations build and quicken in me. He watches and feels my orgasm build and kisses me deeply as I spasm with it and I reach up to wrap my arms around him. The hands withdraw from me and he takes me up and back into the still hot water and washes the oils off. He removes the mask and turns off the jets.

He takes me out of the water, wraps me in a towel and places me gently in the bed, curls around me as we fall asleep.

Photo Shoot

Sea side and sun. Two of the prerequisites to this photo shoot we've spoken about for ages. Today is that day, we got up early to watch the sunrise, the darkness turning to light. The navy blue of the night sky turning to light blue of day as the sun came up along with an increase in my nervousness. I stretched my sleepiness while yawning and making that catlike sound, laughing at him as he shied away, ever saying mind you stretch your lazy on me. I drag out the wrap from the suitcase and we brush our teeth and head to the dining room for breakfast. It was difficult getting this team together, the right models and photographer, finding the right venue that had the backdrop we wanted and getting the props together.

I'm too nervous to eat, but he says, look nuh? If u don't eat now, you might not get another chance to cause you know how you can get when you start something. Laaauuux, I think, he knows me too well and I force myself to eat something and drink my morning caffeine. The others arrive and they're unloading the car of the photographic equipment and their props. Hey guys, come eat something before we start he calls out to them and they troop in, chatting and laughing in preparation of the day. I smile at them and as my heart rate increases, I feel my face begin to flush in anticipation of what was to come.

He has many ideas to put forth, most of them rather intriguing, and well, I'm just here for the ride. I went back to the room to get the 'props', the several pairs of shoes, the skirts, collar and wristlets that he has determined would make great pictures. The photographer and the models have all read the stories so they all have an idea of what we were looking for and what we wanted the photos to depict. We had had discussions at length and they had some great ideas too.

The photographer looks out at the horizon through the balcony, the sea as the backdrop and the greenery in some parts, he nods his head, looking at the light meter and says, hey guys we gotta get a move on while the sun is shining. I blow out the breath I didn't even know I was holding. Am I ready for this??

The photographer looks at me, while his assistant is putting the make-up on my tattoos, hiding my identity so to speak and putting the oil on my body, to make great photos as we had discussed previously, the skirt and the shoes, collar and wristlets in place, he says to me, you do some poses for me, alone at first to begin, let's get everybody in the mood. As I pose in some of the positions we had talked about, he directs from off to the side while the camera whirrs, it's lens and shutter going, the flash and reflectors bouncing the light off me. I look over at him and everything disappears. And I am doing this for him and him alone. I barely hear the others, sounds of approval and directions as they get some really great shots, showing up right away on the laptop. Bend my knee here, place it on the chair, bend my head, move my hair so, twist my hip, place my hand there.

The other guys are preparing to enter the scene and the male model steps in front of me, I look up and up at him, his body all oiled and slick, he has no clothes on, dark skin, hard slender body . . . . I step out of my skirt, remove the collar and wristlets. He turns to face the camera, I step up behind him, my front flush against his back, slightly bending my knees as I reach around with my right hand to cup him. The contrast of his dark skin and my light skin makes some interesting photos. Rhetorically I ask, should I put my leg up around as well? Try the photographer says and my left leg wraps around his, slightly off balance, I anchor myself against him and as my body rubs against his, the model laughs a little self consciously because as my warm oiled hand rubs against him, I can feel him stir a little and I smile.

We had talked about this before, what to do I wonder, I look up to see him watching me intently, that MickeyD grin, almost licking his lips. The oils from my hand and from the models body mix and heat up as the camera takes the photos from different angles, the photographer ever moving, my leg drops to the floor and our bodies glide against each other, my nipples harden from the friction and my fingers begin to twitch as the model rubs himself slightly against my hand. Almost in reflex my fingers tighten around him and he hardens more. What was limp and hanging between his legs when we started has begun to indurate and grow, changing it's orientation. The model looks down at me and I look up into his face, both of us slightly uncomfortable. I smile at him and he clears his throat, and my hand moves to stroke him, from the base upwards. He inhales sharply and does not pull away.

I move my fingers to encircle his girth while moving my hand back down to the base, the oils making the movement slick and friction appears because I'm gripping him tightly. Maintaining eye contact, he begins to move against my hand and I slip around from behind him, still gripping him and moving my hand up and down his shaft.

He, avidly watching, indicates to the photographer, not to stop shooting, as I face the model, I look down at my hand moving up and down, my other hand runs down the models abs and his firm six pack, slick with oil, to cup his scrotum gently. I hear when he groans and feel when he thrusts against my hand, I can feel it through his movements that he is, oh so turned on. I bend my head and take the tip of him into my mouth, swirling my tongue against him, feeling him buck and thrust against me, I continue to move my hand up and down sucking at him, I move my head so that he slides out of my mouth, in and out, up and down with my hand, swirling my tongue and sucking.

I pull him out of my mouth as he stiffens and comes all over my hand and spasms his fluids onto my chest. The model laughs self consciously as I release him and straighten up. I look over at him, me still naked, except for my shoes, another mans come all over me and he smiles so wide, I can see and feel his enjoyment in the moment. And I am so happy to finally bring one of his scenarios to a reality.

Submissive

Role playing he called it. This new thing we have created on our own terms, the dominant/submissive roles. Initially it was just conversations held in fun, The Story of O and other dominant/submissive bits of literature we researched and the web sites we looked at together. The extreme binding, the costumes, the toys, the use by other people and the contracts. I wasn't too sure I was up for this submissive role, being not essentially domineering, still not entirely comfortable giving myself over to the whims and fancies of another. It's all about trust he pointed out. Soooooo, after much talking and to and fro, we agree to try it out, just us to get a feel for it. And we agreed on a safe word. He has said, these roles are best played in public, I said noooooo way, not the first time. Compromise.

Saturday morning, house work day. Never our most happy time, but today, we spice it up a bit. As is usual, he's up before me, and I awaken to see the 'costume' on the bed. This is the beginning of it, the collar and the short black 'maids' skirt, frills and all and those heels, I hope I can walk around in them all day. I smile to myself and get up to brush my teeth and don the collar, skirt and the shoes. He is sitting in the dining room reading the paper, breakfast at the ready, good morning I say, he looks up and down at me and smiles that MickyD grin, coffee is ready. Come here he says, patting his knee, sit here. Oookay, I walk over and sit, drinking my coffee while he strokes my thighs up and down, Lord, I think, how he expect me to drink my coffee with this onslaught of lust he is beginning to stir in me?? My thighs part of their own volition and he pushes his hand up to stroke at my clit, my breathing increases and I begin to feel my juices flow, uuuuugh I groan and he pulls his hand back and returns to stroking my thighs.

After the coffee is done, we both get up and start the cleaning, sweeping up and setting up laundry, obviously I'm not hanging out clothes today. Ever so often he walks over to me, pushes me over the backs of any chair or just bends me over in the midst of whatever I am doing. He fondles me roughly, sometimes, pushing his fingers in, sometimes, a tongue, never bringing me to orgasm and never allowing me to touch him. He knows my frustration levels are rising as he 'tortures' me. At one point he disappears and then walks up behind me and bends me over, spreading my legs apart and caressing my butt and I hear the buzz of the bullet and I groan silently to myself. He pushes it against my clit and I can feel it buzzing against me and involuntarily I begin to move my pelvis, he eases it away just a bit until I stop moving and he repeats the action, bullet on and off, and so it goes, this wanting soooo bad to come, but he won't allow it. I can feel my skin begin to flush and I feel tingly everywhere and still he withholds from me that one tiny push over the edge. And then he leaves. I actually cross my eyes and inhale deeply and have the presence of mind to return to whatever task I was doing, as to how well it was done? Hmmmmmmmmm, I can't remember.

At one point the phone rings and I answer, calling him to it as it was work calling. As I make to move off, he grabs at my hand sitting me down on his lap. While he is conversing with his boss, he pushes his hand up under the skirt and begins to rub at my clit and the piercing, softly at first then harder. I begin to move my pelvis with the rubbing while he talks. He pushes his fingers up into me and rubs at my G-spot and as he ends the call, pulls his fingers out and smiles at me. I stick my tongue out at him as I get up. He raises his eye brow and says, you're gonna pay for that.

Eventually all the chores are finished and he hooks his finger into the ring at the front of the collar leading me into our 'playroom'. He attaches me to the wall with my back to him and binds my hands up and out, he spread apart my feet and ties my ankles so that I am in an erect X-position. And he blindfolds me. I can hear him moving about and then I feel soft touches against my back and thighs, feathery light up and down, between my legs along my arms. It almost begins to feel painful the way it caresses me so lightly. It feels like hours. And then he moves on to harder caresses, using his hands running up and down my limbs soft in some parts, harder in others, he rubs me down with oils and my skin is now slick and super sensitive.

I can feel my clit begin to pulse of it's own volition and I bite my lip to keep from making a sound. He rubs his hand against me and I hear the bullet start up again, and I actually shy away from its contact the way I am sooooo on edge. He pushes his finger in just enough to caress my G-spot and when the bullet makes contact with my clit, I literally explode, squirting onto the floor and down my leg. My finger nails bite into my palms and I spasm again and again. He says mmmmmmmm and moves his hands to rub my inner thighs, smearing me all over me. He grasps at my thighs and pushes his head between my thighs and sucks my clit. I begin to writhe along with the rhythm of his tongue as he sucks and licks at me.

I begin to feel unstable in the shoes as he works his tongue and fingers at me again and again. Rubbing at my G-spot and swirling his tongue. He releases my hands and ankles, but I am still attached to the wall by the collar. He puts his hands on either side of my pelvis pulling me towards him, applying pressure to my neck. I feel when he pushes into me with such force and abandon it indicates that I was not the only one affected by todays doings.

I brace myself against the wall as he thrusts heavily, holding onto my hips with his hands, hard and fast almost violently, until the telltale stiffening, he spills himself into me.

Predator

The room was dark and cool, with recessed lights along the bar, shining their low wattage illumination over the stools placed strategically under them. On the other side of the room were the wall to wall mattresses covered in red satin and filled with naked and half dressed bodies, all intertwined and in constant motion, writhing in the semi-dark barely able to tell where one body ended and the other began. We entered the room, walking slowly, me in my 5-inch high 'hooker' shoes, short black skirt, skimpy top, his hand resting on the small of my back caressing me as he watched the room action.

He stopped by one of the stools and sat on it, opening his thighs and dragging me backwards into the crux of his groin. Leaning against him, balancing on those shoes, I know he is turned on by what is happening in the room, as he watches them avidly. We haven't really decided if we were gonna ditch our clothes and join in, this decision would probably be made as a spur of the moment thing, if the timing is right and the mood grabs us both. It's been something we have talked about countless numbers of times, and we know there is no pressure on either side to do or not to do. This was the reason we chose this time to come here, the activities of the 'swing group', the events they have planned and the freedom and lack of pressure to partake or desist. Everyone so far has been real cool, chatting by the pool, in the dining areas and bars. Some of them even know each other from previous meetings. Tonight is 'red room' night, very similar to the Playboy series we watch all the time.

He orders some red wine for me and a rum and coke for himself and I become immersed in the wine and the room action as well. Watching other people have sex I have found has become something of a turn on for me, and it being not the usual "porn" type sex of daggering, as it was taking place now was quite an erotic thing. I can hear the moans and some screaming, sounds of sucking and penetration, sounds of orgasms, grunts and sounds of pleasure.

He holds his drink in one hand sipping his drink while the other hand is caressing my naked side, then up and down my thigh, under my skirt rubbing at my clit lightly, playing with the piercing and my lips, smearing the inevitable wetness around my thighs and hairless mound. I can feel his evident arousal in the small of my back and I know he has that MickeyD grin plastered on his face. My breathing increases and I can feel my face flush. He takes the glass from my hand and rests it on the bar. Then he grasps my two wrists, bringing them behind me and gets my hands to hold the opposite elbow, gripping them firmly, flat against my spine. With his other hand, he begins a slow light tapping and rubbing of my clit and the piercing and my lips, dipping his finger in ever so often, rubbing at my G-spot. He sucks hard at my neck and I arch my back, he sticks his tongue in my ear. As he arouses me the way he knows how, that familiar wetness soaks his fingers and the fluids hits his hand and runs down my thigh, causing him to groan. I push back against him, closing my eyes, feeling his arousal, hard and insistent against my back. We zone out the room.

I open my eyes as I sense some one coming close to my feet. And I see a silhouette crawling towards my feet braced on the ground, I can't tell if its human or animal and I feel like prey, trapped while the predator comes toward me. I feel when he nods his head and the predator begins to lick at my feet. I gaze at this predator in the semi-darkness as he holds me immobile almost roughly, and the predator begins a slow climb up my left leg with their tongue, he grasps my right thigh bending the knee and bringing it over his thigh, opening me up and still holding my hands behind my back. Licking at my knee, licking my inner thigh, sucking and moving so slowly up my limb, the predator moves and I brace back against him attempting to maintain my balance. I have no idea what to expect. He pulls me hard against him and I feel his tongue in my ear, licking and he moves to my neck. I bend my head to the side while he licks and sucks at my neck.

He releases my thigh and begins a slow caress of my breasts and nipples, tugging and pinching at their erectness almost painfully at times rubbing them between his fingers, building my arousal. My heart begins to pound in my chest. The predator has reached the junction of my thighs and licks lightly at my clit, up and down, swirling the tongue, while he rubs at my breasts, the sensations become almost unbearable. I feel a tongue part my lips and simultaneously he grabs my head, twisting my face to his, plunging his tongue into my mouth, I can taste the rum and I feel that squirt of fluid come out and the predator laps it up avidly while I spasm, groaning into his mouth.

I can hardly maintain my balance as the onslaught begins again, his tongue plunging in and out of my mouth and the predators within my other lips, in and out, hard and soft, licking and sucking at my clit and smearing more of my fluids around my thighs with their tongue. His hand, keeping up the caresses and fondling of my breasts and abdomen, stabilizing the thigh that rests on his, maintaining my openness.

The leg I'm standing on begins to feel unstable and my knee feels most weak. I grab at his midsection behind me, leaning weakly against him and he raises his mouth from mine, releasing my arms. I rest the palms of my hands against his abdomen and I begin to move my leg to the floor. The predator gives me a final hard lick and backs away from us, the same way they had come.

I turn around within the juncture of his thighs, passing my hand lightly against his arousal, resting my head on his shoulder, sighing contentedly as his arms encircle me.

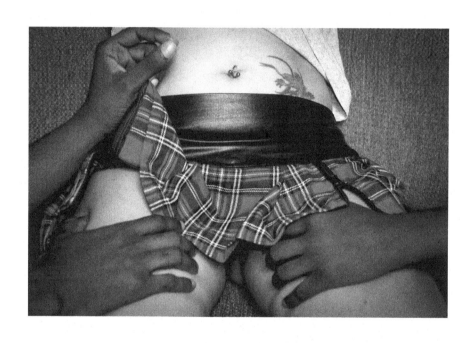

Swing

Half asleep he watches me as I get ready for bed, my usual shower, brushing teeth, combing out my hair. But tonight there is a difference in my routine, instead of coming out the bathroom unclothed, I put on a black silk robe and perfume??? What? he thinks to himself drowsily. Like something out of 'Swing', I walk toward him saying, come nuh? I grasp his hand pulling him out of the bed and we go into the sitting area of the hotel room. The other couple are already there, languishing on opposite ends of the sofa, drinking wine and eating finger food, they await us. We've been meeting for several weeks now, a no pressure kind of thing, getting to know each other and seeing if we were indeed compatible mentally and physically. The other couple have done this before, so it is nothing new to them, it is this newness of our encounter with others that have me nervous. He is of course in seventh heaven, me less so, but we agreed among ourselves, no penetration for this first physical encounter, we would see how it progresses and maybe the next time, but we all four have a synergy between us, it may be that it passes the boundaries set tonight. Or it could fulfill our fantasy requirements and we remain fast friends who have a shared experience.

I walk over to the sofa and sit beside the male, tucking my legs under me, almost in a kneeling position and he pours me a glass of wine, he already knows my preference and what it does to me. He sits beside me on my other side and the female half of the couple is now on the other side of him. They start a conversation about some incident that was in the news that day, he rests his hand on my thigh and the male runs his hand down my other thigh. The male does know of my hesitance in this adventure and he accepts it, I need to come to the acceptance of the event on my own. Knowing it is more about him than it is about me, the couple understand their roles in this, but there is much to be gained in such encounters. We chat and eat some more and I begin to feel mellow as I sip the wine.

The male leans over and brushes his tongue against my neck and I close my eyes, holding the wine glass between my two hands between my knees. He turns slightly to watch us and the female rests her hand on his thigh closest to her, he puts his hand on top of the female's and rubs at the back of it distractedly. The female knows she is not the focus of this encounter for him and she understands it is his fantasy to watch me be pleasured by another.

I tilt my head slightly, opening the access to my neck and subtly giving my acquiescence for the male to proceed. The male takes things slowly, rubbing lightly on my thigh, increasing the pressure in stages and licking my neck, sucking slightly, holding my head with his other hand. My breathing begins to quicken and I open my eyes slightly to see him watching me avidly, a half smile on his face, I reach down to touch his hand that is resting on my thigh and he turns his hand over and clasps mine, intertwining my fingers with his, rubbing his thumb over my wrist. He takes the wine glass from me and rests it on the table.

The male runs his hand up the inside of my thighs, pushing apart my legs slightly and I shift to accommodate this. The male pulls at the ties of the robe and moves his hand to gently rub his fingers against my clit, bending his head, he sucks at my breasts, swirling his tongue around my nipples. And he moves his hand from the females to the small of my back and begins to caress me there, I close my eyes and all the sensations from the both of them become more acute. The male moves to kneel in front of me and pushing my knees apart until I am almost kneeling, dips his finger tips into me softly, I inhale sharply and he bends his head, tonguing my clit. Slowly and gently at first, then building up in pressure he sucks at it. Moving his tongue around it and the piercing, the sensations build within me and I begin to move my pelvis. My grip on his hand tighten and I can still feel him caressing my back and I feel when he shifts on the sofa to face me and he kisses me softly on the side of my face.

The male pushes two of his fingers up into me and begins to move them in and out with the rhythm of my movement and they become wet with my juices. My breathing becomes more laboured and my movements more frantic. He moves his lips from my face to suck hard at my neck and caresses my breasts, watching the play of expressions on my face as I flush and spasm as I orgasm. I open my eyes and look at him as he rubs his hand still on my back, flushed and gripping at his hand.

And he wakes up still grasping at my hand as I get into the bed, turns toward me, enfolds me into his arms, still existing in the dream.